# Nessie needs new glasses

By A.K Paterson

First published in Great Britain in 2009
by W.F Graham (Northampton) Ltd
for Lomond Books Ltd, Broxburn, EH52 5NF

ISBN 9781842041215

For many hundreds of years Nessie, the Loch Ness Monster had lived at the bottom of the loch. When she was just a little monster Nessie found that her eyesight wasn't very good. She needed glasses to help her see better. Her good friends, the seals, made Nessie a splendid pair of spectacles.

Nessie could do all the things she wanted. She could read her books, watch the television and play on her computer. She was also the champion goal scorer for her local underwater football team, which is quite something when the goalie has 8 arms!

From all over the world people came to Loch Ness to try and catch a glimpse of the famous Nessie. Most of the time she kept out of sight. But every now and again she teased them!

One day a fierce storm hit the loch. Once the storm was over, Nessie found that her glasses had been broken. She couldn't see at all well!

The seals tried to help Nessie get around the loch. They tried their best but Nessie was very sad. Without her glasses she just couldn't do any of the things she had enjoyed before.

In the middle of the night Nessie had an idea. She needed to get help. Nessie decided to leave the loch and look for her relatives. "Maybe they can lend me the money to buy some glasses!" thought Nessie.

It was very dark when Nessie waved goodbye to her friends. She quietly paddled down the river, past the city of Inverness.

Nessie swam a long way in the North Sea. She thought she could see her cousin, Jimmy, in the distance. "Jimmy, Jimmy!", shouted Nessie, but Jimmy ignored her. "He always was an oily wee man!" thought Nessie as she swam on.

Nessie found it easier to swim, but she could also walk. She headed inland and caught a glimpse of her Auntie Charie. Nessie cried out but Auntie Charie didn't reply! "She must have gone up in the world." said Nessie.

She found her way back to the sea.
Nessie became very excited to see her favourite Uncle Fitlike near the beach in Aberdeen. "I know he has had his ups and downs over the years, but he'll help me out." thought Nessie. No reply! "Maybe he doesn't recognise me. He hasn't seen me for 850 years!" Nessie swam on.

Nessie did her best to make her way down the river near Pitlochry, but it was very hard going because she kept on being hit by flying objects. "Ow! It's like being slapped in the face by a wet fish!" thought Nessie.

She swam up the Firth of Forth near Edinburgh. "Uncle George! Uncle George!" shouted Nessie. Uncle George didn't react. "Maybe he can't hear me over the noise of those trains!"

Nessie took to walking again. She found herself caught up in a big festival parade and a man stuck a number on her! "Why did he call me a float?" wondered Nessie as she won First Prize!

Before she could get her hands on the year's supply of Edinburgh Rock, a loud noise frightened Nessie and she ran away.

Back in the water, Nessie saw her cousin, Big Tom.

"Ouch! Tom always played a bit rough!" said Nessie.

Nessie took to the road again. As she neared Stirling, Nessie saw her Uncle Wally. "He's even taller than I remember!" thought Nessie. "Uncle Wally, Uncle Wally!" "Maybe he can't hear me all the way up there!"

Nessie began to feel rather sad. "What have I done to them?" she asked herself. "Is it because I haven't phoned for 700 years?"

She headed down the Clyde. Nessie had heard that her relatives in Glasgow were very friendly. "Not all that friendly then!" shouted Nessie at her Auntie Neccy, who refused to speak to her.

Near Greenock, Nessie spied her second cousin, Mary. Mary ignored her as well! "You always were stuck up!" shouted Nessie.

Swimming past Ayr, Nessie shouted out to Uncle Humphrey. He didn't shout back. "Huffy Humphrey!" roared Nessie.

Nessie was very upset that all her relatives had ignored her pleas for help. She decided to make her way back home to Loch Ness. "At least the seals will be happy to see me." thought Nessie. "Even if I can't see them!" Nessie was feeling a bit sorry for herself.

Somehow the seals had managed to get word to the people of Inverness that Nessie needed their help. The Invernessians held a huge bring and buy sale to try and raise money for her new glasses.

The Nessie appeal reached its target!

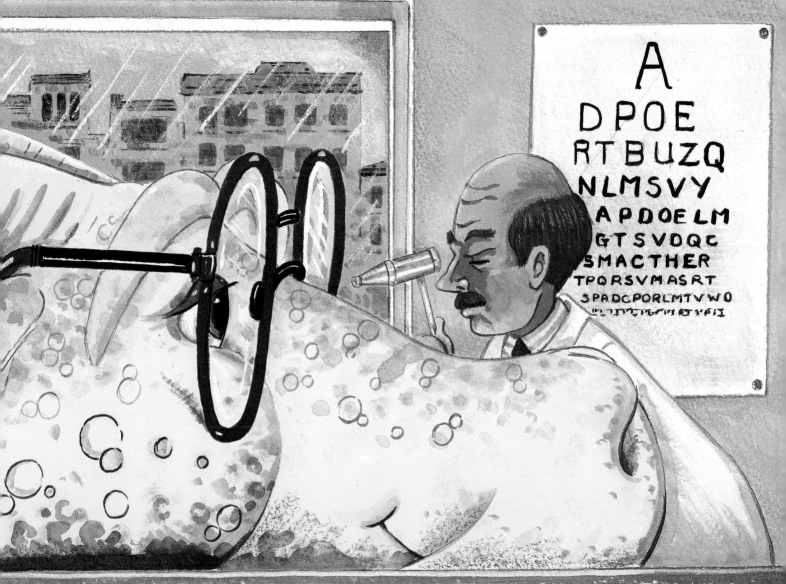

The new glasses were quickly made and Nessie visited the optician in Inverness to have them fitted.

Nessie was very proud of her beautiful new glasses! "I wish all of my relatives could see me now!", she laughed.